Chapter One

Oh no!
Today was the day.
The dreaded day!
The *really* dreaded day!
Today was…

BATH DAY!

"Gerald!" called Mum. "It's that time of year again. Get ready for your bath."

Gerald didn't like bath day. Not one little bit. Being all washed and clean?

THE MONSTER WHO
WAS FEARED OF

**The item should be returned or renewed
by the last date stamped below.**

Dylid dychwelyd neu adnewyddu'r eitem erbyn
y dyddiad olaf sydd wedi'i stampio isod.

To renew visit / Adnewyddwch ar
www.newport.gov.uk/libraries

BLOOMSBURY EDUCATION
LONDON OXFORD NEW YORK NEW DELHI SYDNEY

BLOOMSBURY EDUCATION

Bloomsbury Publishing Plc

50 Bedford Square, London, WC1B 3DP, UK

29 Earlsfort Terrace, Dublin 2, Ireland

BLOOMSBURY, BLOOMSBURY EDUCATION and the Diana logo
are trademarks of Bloomsbury Publishing Plc

First published in Great Britain in 2022 by Bloomsbury Publishing Plc

A catalogue record for this book is available from the British Library

ISBN: PB: 978-1-4729-9454-7; ePDF: 978-1-4729-9455-4; ePub: 978-1-4729-9453-0;
Enhanced ePub: 978-1-8019-9037-0

2 4 6 8 10 9 7 5 3 1

Text design by Sarah Malley

Printed and bound in China by Leo Paper Products, Heshan, Guangdong

To find out more about our authors and books visit www.bloomsbury.com
and sign up for our newsletters

Yuck! It was really, really horrible.
He heard Mum's footsteps coming
up the stairs.
"Eek!" thought Gerald. "I need a
plan and I need it NOW!"
"I'll pretend to be fast asleep,"
he thought.

5

He dived into bed and pulled the
blankets over himself.
"Hmm, but Mum would just
wake me up."

He jumped out of bed and got down on his hands and knees.

"I'll hide under the bed," thought Gerald.

"Hmm, but there might be a scary child hiding under there."

Footsteps were coming closer to his bedroom door.

Then the door swung open and...

"Gerald!" said Mum.
"Bath time. Now."

With a grunt and a grump and a grouch and a groan, Gerald slumped towards the bathroom.
"I've got a surprise for you," said Mum.

"What?" said Gerald.
"Look in the bathroom," said Mum.

"Go on. Open the door."
So, Gerald slowly pushed
open the door... and his
eyes popped wide in shock.

Chapter Two

There was a child inside.

"**Eek!**" cried Gerald. "It's a child!"

"Hello," said the child. "I'm Maggie."

"**EEK!**" said Gerald again.

"I saw the advert," said Maggie, "and I'm here to help you with your bath."
"Advert?" said Gerald, looking at Maggie and feeling very unsure.
"What advert?"
"This advert," said Maggie.

WANTED!

Expert **monster-tamer** needed for yearly bath time.
Must show the monster who is boss.

Duties include:
- Wrestling monster into bath
- Washing monster
- Wrestling monster out of bath
- Drying monster
- Drying bathroom

Good luck!

To apply, contact
Gerald's mum.

Gerald looked at Maggie. Maggie
looked at Gerald.
And Gerald decided there was only
one thing for it:

RUN!

He hurtled across the hallway...

but so did Maggie.

Skedaddled down the stairs...

but so did Maggie.

Crashed through the kitchen...

but so did Maggie.

"No-one else has ever chased me this fast before!" thought Gerald, with a wibbly-wobbly feeling in his tummy. He quickly opened the back door and bounded for the garden, as fast as his furry legs could carry him.

But Maggie came marching
towards him.
"I will NOT have my bath time!"
said Gerald. "I will not use soap.
I will not be clean! So there!"

He trampled through the vegetable
patch, crawled underneath a bush
and hid behind a big tree.
He peeped around the trunk.
There was silence.

"You WILL have your bath time,"
said Maggie, walking towards
him, "because I am an expert
monster-tamer and I always
show the monster who is boss."
"No, I will not have my bath time."

"Yes, you will."

"Why?" said Gerald. He narrowed his eyes at her.

"Because," said Maggie, with a smile, "you will want to."

"Why?" said Gerald again.

"Because," said Maggie, with an even bigger smile, "I have a secret surprise." Then she walked back into the house.

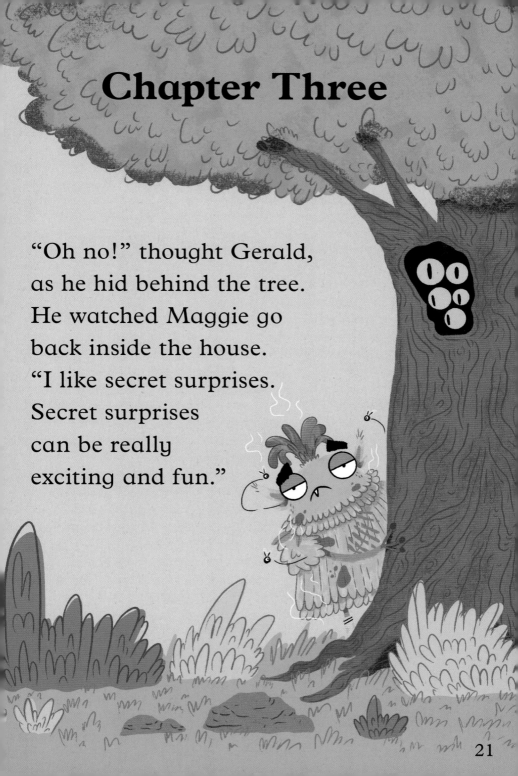

Chapter Three

"Oh no!" thought Gerald,
as he hid behind the tree.
He watched Maggie go
back inside the house.
"I like secret surprises.
Secret surprises
can be really
exciting and fun."

He looked at himself covered in cake
mixture and twigs and bird nests.
That wasn't really exciting and fun.
Suddenly, the bathroom window opened.

"Hurry up!" said Maggie. "The secret surprise is waiting!"

A bird frowned and flew off from Gerald's head. Gerald folded his arms crossly. A dollop of cake mixture landed on his foot. Then he looked up at the bathroom window and gasped.

23

"Wait!" he said.
"Bubbles? Are those
bubbles I can see?"
Gerald's face lit up
and he darted
for the back door.

He crashed through the kitchen,
dashed up the stairs and hurtled
through the hallway...

Until he skidded to a halt at the bathroom.

"Wow!" said Gerald and stared at the bath. There were bubbles everywhere!

"Want to get in?" asked Maggie.

"No!" said Gerald and folded his arms. But he looked at the bubbles. "They look good fun," he thought. "Really good fun."
"There's another secret surprise," said Maggie.

Gerald couldn't help himself. He clapped his huge, furry paws together. "Another one? What?" he said. "This," said Maggie. And she showed him a rubber duck... a pirate boat... a waterwheel and... a mini monster!

That was it! Gerald could not resist
any longer. He dived into the water
with a ginormous…

SPLASH!

Maggie was completely drenched.

"Look what I can do!" squeaked
Gerald in delight. He sent a spout
of water flying into the air from the
monster toy.

He did it again and again, making a
big puddle on the floor.

"I knew you would want your bath,"
said Maggie. "Oh, but don't forget,
you need to wash."
Gerald stopped mid-squirt. "I'm
absolutely not having a wash."

"You are going to have a wash," said
Maggie.
"I am not going to have a wash."
"That's what YOU think," said
Maggie and she smiled.

Chapter Four

"I am NOT going to have a wash,"
said Gerald.
"You ARE."
"No, I'm not."
"You really are," said Maggie.

"BUT I HATE SOAP!" wailed Gerald. "Soap is horrible and clean and... horrible!"
"Well, just pretend it isn't soap," said Maggie.
"How can I do that?" wailed Gerald.

URGH!

Maggie showed him a bottle of green gloop. "Let's pretend this is the slimiest... stinkiest... stickiest troll bogey in the whole wide world!" Gerald frowned at the soap. "Hmm, I'm not sure."

"Try it," said Maggie and squirted on
a great big SPLAT.

SPLAT!

"Aaaargh! My fur!" Gerald gasped.
"What have you done to my fur?"

Maggie put a mirror in front of his face and Gerald laughed.

Then they made funny hairstyles...

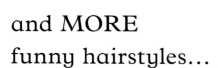

and more funny hairstyles...

and MORE funny hairstyles...

... and then gave his fur a really good scrub until the bubbles disappeared.

"This is the best troll bogey in the world," said Gerald.

"I bet you can't pour a jugful of water over your head," said Maggie.
"Yes, I can!" said Gerald.
"No, you can't."
"Yes, I can!" said Gerald. And he did.

"Well, I think it must be nearly time for your bedtime story," said Maggie. "You'd better get out of the bath." Gerald looked at her and folded his arms. "I'm not getting out of the bath."

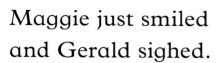

Maggie just smiled
and Gerald sighed.
"I AM going to get out of the bath,
aren't I?" he said. "Tell me. Why
exactly am I going to get out
of the bath?"

TROLL BOGEYS

"Because," said Maggie, "I have one more secret surprise. Close your eyes. And no peeping."

Chapter Five

Gerald closed his eyes and held his breath. What would the secret surprise be?

"You can open them now!" said Maggie.

Gerald opened his eyes and he saw…

GASP!

The softest, fluffiest, pink slippers and bath towel.

"Wow!" he yelled.

He leapt out of the bath with a whoop of delight and soon he was snuggled from head to tail.

Gerald got himself dry in record time and slipped into his pyjamas.

Maggie handed him a small towel. "Please would you wipe the water up from the floor?" she said.
"Of course," said Gerald politely.
"I would be happy to help." And he cleared up the mess.

Maggie handed Gerald's mum the advert with all the jobs ticked off. "Well," said Maggie, "I think that's my job done now. Shall I come back next year?"

"**NO!**" said Gerald.
Maggie and Gerald's mum
looked puzzled.

"**PLEASE** come back tomorrow!"